HIC! HIC? HIC! HIC? HIC! HIC? HIC! HIC?
HIC! HIC? HIC! HIC? HIC! HIC? HIC! HIC?
HIC? HIC! HIC? HIC! HIC? HIC! HIC? HIC!
HIC! HIC? HIC! HIC? HIC! HIC? HIC! HIC?
HIC? HIC! HIC? HIC! HIC? HIC! HIC? HIC!
HIC! HIC? HIC! HIC? HIC! HIC? HIC! HIC?
HIC? HIC! HIC? HIC! HIC? HIC! HIC? HIC!
HIC! HIC? HIC! HIC! HIC! HIC? HIC! HIC?
HIC? HIC! HIC? HIC! HIC? HIC! HIC? HIC!
HIC! HIC? HIC! HIC? HIC! HIC? HIC! HIC?
HIC? HIC! HIC? HIC! HIC? HIC! HIC? HIC!
HIC! HIC? HIC! HIC? HIC! HIC? HIC! HIC?

With special thanks to Ekkehard Loewen

This book has been printed on a Risograph. This eco-friendly printing system uses organic, soy-based inks, and combines the technology of screen printing with a photocopier machine. The colours are transparent, so they interact with each other, and the result is a unique textural experience. Each page can turn out a little differently, so no two books are identical. The printed pages are hand bound in our book making workshop.

Hic!
Copyright © 2017 Tara Books Private Limited

For the text: Anushka Ravishankar
For the illustrations: Christiane Pieper
Design: Ragini Siruguri

For this edition:
Tara Publishing Ltd., UK <www.tarabooks.com/uk>
and
Tara Books Private Ltd., India <www.tarabooks.com>

Production: C. Arumugam
Printed in India by AMM Screens, Chennai

ISBN: 978-93-83145-64-5

HIC?

Anushka Ravishankar and Christiane Pieper

Drink a pail of water, standing on a brick.

Put some mustard in your nose,

which then, proceed to lick.

Shout AWALLAGULLAGABUGGAMUGGACHICK!

...HIC?!

Spin round and round, just like a top
Until you're feeling sick.

Stand up on your head
          and then recite a limerick.

Tie a ribbon round your nose
and spell **C-A-C-O-P-H-O-N-I-C.**

and breathe out very quick.

Eat twelve carrots, sixteen beans

and one cinnamon stick.

EIGHT WAYS
TO GET RID OF
HICCUPS

Want to know how
to get rid of hiccups?
Read this book!
WARNING: it might not work.

Okay, do you have better ideas

on how to stop hiccups?

HIC! HIC? HIC! HIC? HIC! HIC? HIC! HIC?

HIC! HIC? HIC! HIC? HIC! HIC? HIC! HIC?

HIC? HIC! HIC? HIC! HIC? HIC! HIC? HIC!

HIC! HIC? HIC! HIC? HIC! HIC? HIC! HIC?

HIC? HIC! HIC? HIC! HIC? HIC! HIC? HIC!

HIC! HIC? HIC! HIC? HIC! HIC? HIC! HIC?

HIC? HIC! HIC? HIC! HIC? HIC! HIC? HIC!

HIC! HIC? HIC! HIC? HIC! HIC? HIC! HIC?

HIC? HIC! HIC? HIC! HIC? HIC! HIC? HIC!

HIC! HIC? HIC! HIC? HIC! HIC? HIC! HIC?

HIC? HIC! HIC? HIC! HIC? HIC! HIC? HIC!

HIC! HIC? HIC! HIC? HIC! HIC? HIC! HIC?